Ribbit!

Written by
Rodrigo
Folgueira

Illustrated by
Poly
Bernatene

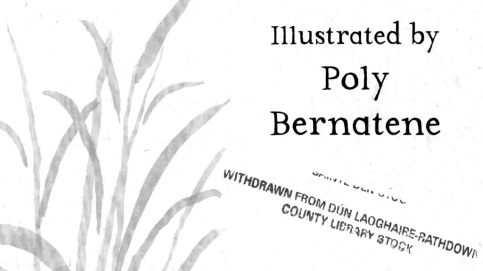

This book is
dedicated to friendship,
especially ours

Rodrigo and Poly

First published in 2012
by Meadowside Children's Books
185 Fleet Street, London, EC4A 2HS
www.meadowsidebooks.com

Text © Rodrigo Folgueira
Illustrations © Poly Bernatene
The rights of Rodrigo Folgueira and Poly Bernatene
to be identified as the author and illustrator of this
work have been asserted by them in accordance with
the Copyright, Designs and Patents Act, 1988

A CIP catalogue record for this book
is available from the British Library
10 9 8 7 6 5 4 3 2 1

Printed in China

meadowside
CHILDREN'S BOOKS

Once upon a time,

there was a pond which was home to a family of frogs.

It was their pond, and they were very happy living there.

But, one morning,
they discovered
a surprise visitor...

It was a pig -

a little pink pig - sitting on a rock.

"**Goodness!**" said the frogs.
"Why is there a pig in our pond?"

They whispered amongst themselves,
until finally the chief frog spoke up:

"Ahem. Good morning.
What can we do for you?"

And, to their amazement,
the little pig answered...

"Ribbit!"

"WHAT did he say?"
cried the frogs.
"This pig is confused!"
"Does he think he's a frog?"
"Is he making fun of us?"

But again, all the little pig said was...

"Ribbit!"

News of the little pig who thought he
was a frog spread fast, and all the animals
hurried to the pond to see the visitor.

"This new relative of
yours is a little **pink!**"
said the raccoon.

"He's no relation of ours!"
said the frogs.

"He certainly **sounds** like a frog..."
said the weasel.
"Why would a pig **want** to be a frog?"
asked the parrot.

"And what's wrong with
being a frog, may we ask?"
exclaimed the frogs.

Everyone started
shouting at each other,
completely ignoring the little pig...

who just sat there, practising his

"Ribbit!"

The animals laughed **and laughed** –
and the frogs got angrier **and angrier** –
until, finally, the chief frog shouted out...

"Stop!"

"We're not getting anywhere by fighting!
We must go and find the wise old beetle.
He'll know what to do."

"The wise old beetle?"
gasped all the animals.

"He hates to
be disturbed!"

"I know," said the chief frog.
"But this is very serious."

"That's true," said the animals.

And off they went.

And the little pig said...

"Ribbit?"

The animals found the wise old beetle, and tried to explain the problem.

It was hard for him to understand,
because they were all talking at once.
In the end he agreed to go with
them to the pond.

But when they arrived...

"Where did
the pig go?"
the animals cried.

"Who was he?"

"What did he
want?"

"Maybe," said the wise old beetle,
"He just wanted to make
new friends."

And off he went.

"Oh dear!" said the animals.

They hadn't thought of that!

"Tweet!"

And, sure enough, high up in
a tree nearby, the animals found
the little pig. He was still trying
to make new friends.

And why not – after all...

"Tweet!"

"Tweet!"

"Tweet!"

"Tweet!"

"Tweet!"

"Tweet!"

"Tweet!"

"Tweet!"

"Tweet!"

"Tweet!"

"Tweet!"

...making
new friends
can be fun!